DISNEY·PIXAR

TOY STORY

DISNEY LEARNING

HOW TO BE A BELOVED TOY

TEAMWORK WITH WOODY

Jennifer Boothroyd

Lerner Publications ◆ Minneapolis

For Claire and Gavin

Lerner Publications Company
A division of Lerner Publishing Group, Inc.
241 First Avenue North
Minneapolis, MN 55401 USA

For reading levels and more information, look up this title at www.lernerbooks.com.

Main body text set in Mikado a 14.5/22.
Typeface provided by HVD Fonts.

Library of Congress Cataloging-in-Publication Data

Names: Boothroyd, Jennifer, 1972– author.
Title: How to be a beloved toy : teamwork with Woody / Jennifer Boothroyd.
Description: Minneapolis : Lerner Publications, [2019] | Series: Disney great character
    guides | Audience: Age: 6–10. | Audience: K to Grade 3. | Includes bibliographical
    references.
Identifiers: LCCN 2018024092 (print) | LCCN 2018037807 (ebook) | ISBN 9781541543119
    (eb pdf) | ISBN 9781541539051 (lb : alk. paper) | ISBN 9781541545991 (pb : alk.
    paper)
Subjects: LCSH: Teams in the workplace—Juvenile literature. | Critical thinking—
    Juvenile literature. | Toys—Juvenile literature.
Classification: LCC HD66 (ebook) | LCC HD66 .B666 2019 (print) | DDC 658.4/022—
    dc23

LC record available at https://lccn.loc.gov/2018024092

Manufactured in the United States of America
1-45088-35915-9/6/2018

Table of Contents

The Right Candidate

Toys have brought comfort and joy to children throughout history. A career as a beloved toy is full of tradition and new opportunities. It is one of the most important jobs in the world.

Toys must focus on the well-being of their kid, but this career has many perks. Beloved toys enjoy hours of playtime and laughter. They get a comfortable place to sleep and often get carried everywhere they go. Best of all, they are loved by their kids.

Becoming a beloved toy is not for everyone. The best candidates are creative problem solvers. They cooperate with others and like to be part of a team. They know that to do their jobs well, they can't put themselves first.

Toys need to be mentally and physically tough. They can't fall apart from being hugged thousands of times or get bored lying still for hours. Of course, being able to put up with dog or toddler slobber is good too!

A Toy's Life

Woody is Andy's favorite toy. Woody's job is to take care of Andy. He goes on imaginative adventures with Andy. He listens when Andy needs someone to talk to. He also cares about the other toys. He knows his job is important and always tries to do his best.

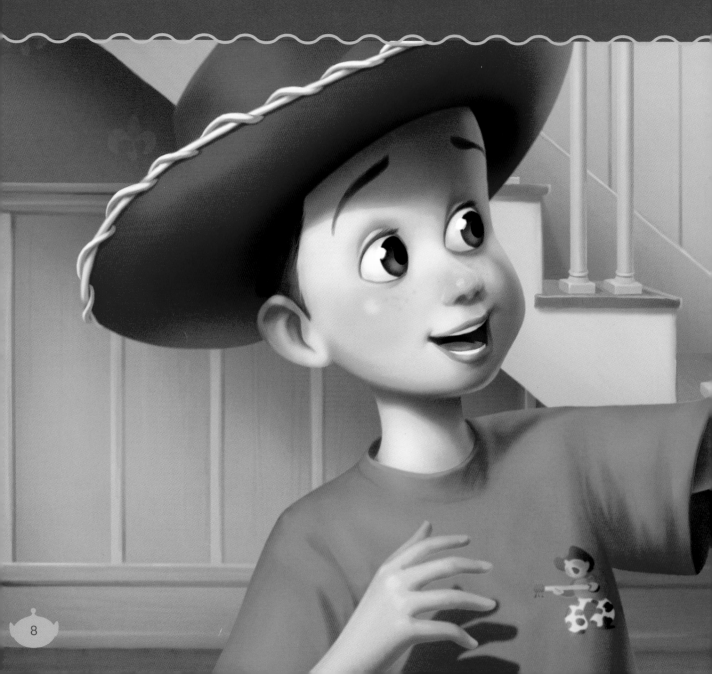

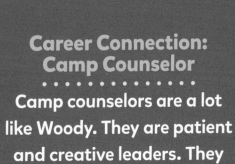

**Career Connection:
Camp Counselor**
· · · · · · · · · · · · ·
Camp counselors are a lot
like Woody. They are patient
and creative leaders. They
care about their campers.
Camp counselors work hard
to help kids have a great
time at camp.

Did You Know?
· · · · · · · · · · · · ·
Toy Story was the first feature-length
computer-animated film. It was
released in 1995.

Woody and his friends must lie completely still if people are around. When people can't see them, Andy's toys move around and talk to one another. "It doesn't matter how much we're played with," Woody tells the others. "What matters is that we're here for Andy when he needs us. That's what we're made for, right?"

Character Callout

Woody and the other toys are patient. They wait without complaining until they are needed on the job.

Finding Your Place on the Team

For his birthday, Andy gets a Buzz Lightyear toy. Woody tries to welcome him to Andy's room. But things don't go very well when he realizes that Buzz thinks he's a real space ranger, not a toy.

All the toys are impressed with Buzz—except for Woody. Buzz shows his flying skills by jumping off Andy's bed. He bounces on a ball, sails down a race car track, and spins around the ceiling before landing back on Andy's bed.

"That wasn't flying. That was falling with style!" Woody complains.

Buzz is now a big part of playtime with Andy. Andy writes his name on Buzz's shoe. He's officially a part of the team.

Woody can't help but feel jealous. He feels worried that Andy may play with Buzz more than with him. Woody doesn't want to lose his place as Andy's favorite toy—or as leader of the team.

"I know Andy's excited about Buzz," Bo Peep tells Woody. "But you know he'll always have a special place for you."

NOT A FLYING TOY

Did You Know?

Even though a light-year sounds like a measurement of time, it is actually a measurement of distance. It measures how far light in space travels in one year.

One day, Woody and Buzz get lost outside. Sid, a tough neighbor kid, takes them to his house. As they sneak out of the house, Buzz sees a Buzz Lightyear toy commercial. Buzz gets upset when he realizes he is actually a toy. "A stupid, little, insignificant toy," he says sadly.

"Wait a minute," Woody says. "Being a toy is a lot better than being a space ranger. Look, over in that house is a kid who thinks you are the greatest, and it's not because you are a space ranger, pal. It's because you're a toy. You are *his* toy."

Woody knows Buzz is important to Andy. He's willing to work with Buzz if it means making Andy happy.

Buzz thinks about what Woody has said. He looks at Andy's name on the bottom of his boot. Buzz realizes being a toy *is* an important job. "Come on, Sheriff. There's a kid that needs us," he says.

Together, they make their way back to Andy. Andy is happy he found his favorite toys. The other toys are happy the whole team is back together.

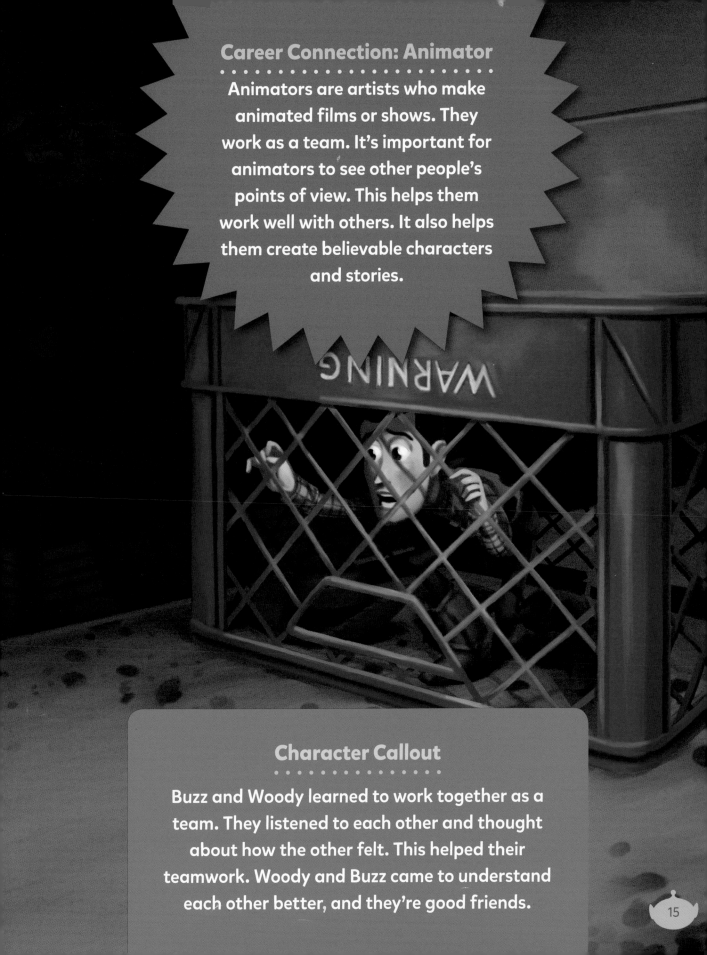

Career Connection: Animator

Animators are artists who make animated films or shows. They work as a team. It's important for animators to see other people's points of view. This helps them work well with others. It also helps them create believable characters and stories.

Character Callout

Buzz and Woody learned to work together as a team. They listened to each other and thought about how the other felt. This helped their teamwork. Woody and Buzz came to understand each other better, and they're good friends.

It's Tough to Be a Toy

Later, Andy goes away to camp. His mom has a garage sale. Woody rescues a toy from the sale but gets trapped outside. While Andy's mom is distracted, a toy collector takes Woody.

At the collector's home, Woody learns he was the star of a famous TV show. He meets his TV show friends: Jessie the Yodeling Cowgirl, Stinky Pete the Prospector, and Woody's horse, Bullseye. Together, they make up the Roundup Gang!

Jessie is excited. The Roundup Gang toys have been sold to a toy museum in Japan!

"I can't go to Japan. I've got to get back to Andy," Woody insists.

"The museum is only interested in the collection if you're in it, Woody," the Prospector explains.

Woody doesn't know what to do. His job is to help Andy, but he doesn't want to let his new friends down. How can he make the right choice?

Did You Know?
. . . .
There is a National Museum of Play in Rochester, New York. Visitors can experience different ways to play and see the National Toy Hall of Fame.

Meanwhile, Andy's toys find out who took Woody. They sneak out to rescue him. It's a dangerous mission, but the toys know they must get their friend back. They need him, and Andy does too!

Character Callout

Buzz and the other toys were resourceful as they rescued Woody. They used technology to figure out who took him. They wore disguises to stay safe, and they weren't afraid to ask for help from other toys.

The toys find Woody, but he doesn't want to go back to Andy's. He says that he can't abandon the Roundup Gang. "They need me to get into a museum," he explains. "Without me, they go back into storage—maybe forever."

"Woody, you're not a collector's item," Buzz says. "You are a *toy*! Somewhere in that pad of stuffing is a toy who taught me that life's only worth living if you're being loved by a kid."

Woody remembers that his job is to be there for Andy.
"This is what it's all about, to make a child happy,"
he tells the Roundup Gang. He asks them to come to
Andy's house with him.

21

Safe at Andy's, the toys agree to never leave Andy until he doesn't need them anymore. Buzz asks Woody if he's worried about Andy growing up.

"Nah," Woody says. "It'll be fun while it lasts."

Environmental scientists study the natural world and the impact humans have on the planet. They figure out the best ways to use and conserve Earth's resources. Talk about being resourceful!

WELCOME Home ANDY

When Your Kid Grows Up

Many years have passed, and Andy is going away to college. He hasn't played with his toys in a long time. Andy decides to bring Woody with him and put the others in the attic. Unfortunately, there's a mix-up. Woody and the toys get donated to a daycare center.

Some of the toys decide to stay to help the children at the center. Woody leads the others back to Andy's house. Buzz, Jessie, and the other toys get ready to be put into storage. They'll be okay as long as they have one another. Woody gets ready to go off to college with Andy.

Character Callout

Woody has learned to be selfless. He knows part of his job is putting the needs of others before his wants. He does what's best for the common good, even though it might not be easy.

But Woody thinks about what it means to be a toy. He remembers a girl named Bonnie from the daycare. She's a special kid with a great imagination who loves her toys. Woody leaves a note on the box of toys and climbs in with his friends. Andy thinks his mom wrote the note, so he follows the directions to Bonnie's house.

Did You Know?
· · · · · · · · · · · · · ·
Donating old toys helps the environment. It keeps them from being thrown in the trash, and it gives someone else a chance to play with them. Too much trash pollutes Earth's air, land, and water.

Bonnie's mom has known Andy since he was young. Andy shows Bonnie the toys and tells her about each of them. "Someone told me you're really good with toys," he says. "These are mine, but I'm going away now so I need someone really special to play with them."

He pauses when he gets to Woody. "Woody's been my pal as long as I can remember. The thing that makes Woody special is that he'll never give up on you, ever. He'll be there for you no matter what." Andy and Bonnie imagine a fun adventure together. The toys are thrilled to play with Andy one last time.

"Now you gotta promise to take good care of these guys. They mean a lot to me," Andy tells Bonnie. As he leaves, Bonnie helps Woody wave goodbye.

"Thanks, guys," Andy says to his toys before he drives away. He appreciates how they helped him through the years.

Career Connection: Teacher

Teachers work hard for their students. They care about their students even though they will go to a new class next year. This may make teachers sad, but just like Woody, they know it's important to help their kids grow.

The toys are grateful Andy loved them enough to give them to Bonnie. They know she will take good care of them. These beloved toys are ready for their next assignment. They will be there for Bonnie whenever she needs them.

All in a Day's Work

Andy's toys work as a team to solve problems. What are the hard parts of working as a team? What are the best parts of working as a team?

When did you do something selfless? Was it a hard choice? How did you feel afterward?

"We always said this job isn't about getting played with. It's about . . ."
–Woody

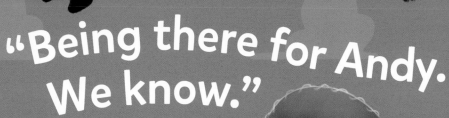

"Being there for Andy. We know."
–Jessie

Glossary

beloved: much loved

candidate: someone who is seeking a job

conserve: to avoid wasteful or destructive use

cooperate: to work together

environment: the natural world

insignificant: meaningless

mission: an important assignment

tradition: a way of doing something that has been used for a very long time

To Learn More

Books

Lindeen, Mary. *Toy Story Top 10s: To Infinity and Beyond*. Minneapolis: Lerner Publications, 2019.
Read all about the top moments from the Toy Story movies.

Paul, Miranda. *Whose Hands Are These? A Community Helper Guessing Book*. Minneapolis: Millbrook Press, 2016.
Discover different jobs of workers that help their community.

Websites

Disney Pixar: Toy Story
https://toystory.disney.com/
Visit this website to dive into the world of Toy Story.

The Pros and Cons of Being a Toy
https://ohmy.disney.com/movies/2015/06/28/the-pros-and
-cons-of-being-a-toy/
Explore the benefits and the challenges toys face every day.